WITHDRAWN

HIS DIRTY SECRET 10

SIDE CHICK CONFESSIONS BOOK 10

MIA BLACK

D0063150

Copyright © 2018 Mia Black

All rights reserved. This book or any portion thereof may
not be reproduced or used in any manner whatsoever
without the express written permission of the publisher

Jayla

It was dark, and I was afraid. My heart was pounding fast, and my breathing was still quick. I had to be quiet, but I was so scared that I couldn't do much of anything. I mean, it's not like I had much of a choice. What the fuck was I doing with my life? I was supposed to be getting away from the drama and now everywhere I go, I was knee deep in some bull-shit. I mean, is it me? Do I just attract drama? Does drama just follow me wherever I go?

My life and my life choices started to flash before my eyes. Every stupid decision I made played back in my head. How could I be so dumb? Every time I think I've fallen for someone, something dangerous happens. I was supposed to come here and avoid all that shit but no, I didn't. Somehow, I have ended up in an even more dangerous situation. The tears started all over again and I hated myself for it. It was natural for me to cry, but I was so afraid that I would be heard and who knows what will happen to me?

Everything was fine before I decided to hook up with Shane. I was in this closet and it looked like my life is coming to an end. What's going to happen to Keon? What's going to happen to my little sister? There is so much that I wanted to do, but it looked like that was over. I was gone.

CHAPTER 1

Damiah

The feel of the weed smoke coming out my lips made me happy every single time. Yeah shit was a little fucked up between me and Shane, but that was going to be dealt with soon. Right now, it was about me and my baddest bitch, Britanya, kickin it together.

"Damn bitch, you just gonna keep the weed all to yourself?" she complained, reaching out. "You said you wanted to split the shit, not take it all for yourself. You always was a greedy motherfucker," she laughed.

"Girl, you know that this is my medicine. I need this shit." I smiled, meaning every word.

"What's going on with you?" I reached over and handed her the weed.

"What else girl?   Bitch ass niggas." We both laughed.   "Ever since I started messing with Will, shit been different."

"What you mean?   You and that nigga been on and off forever.   Why should shit be different now?"

"Well you know we've been fucking with no title for like years and I was cool with that."

"Uh huh?" I stretched out my hand for the weed.   She gave it back to me and I took one long pull. "So, what's up?" I replied as I blew the smoke out my nose.

"He's the one that said that we need to stop playing games and that we need to be official." She rolled her eyes.   "All of that bullshit."

"Right, I remember when you told me that. So, what's up?"

"Now all of a sudden, he's acting like a bitch.   He's blowing up my phone to see where I am.   He's calling to check up on me.   The fuck? It's like he thinks I'm his property. I don't want that shit."

"You know dudes be trippin."

"For real. Like just the other day he asked me to pay for dinner."

"He did not!" I laughed, choking on the smoke. "This motherfucker about to kill me." I handed her the weed. "What did you say?"

"I asked him if he was broke and he got mad. I think that's a good question to ask. Only a broke bum ass nigga would ask a female to pay. I had to end that situation. That's why I like playing with these dudes. Let me get my fix, get my bread, a little bit of dick, and I will keep it moving. I don't got time for no broke ass dude."

I nodded my head. Even though Shane could be a bitch, he never asked me to pay for anything. He always spent money on me and made sure I had money in my pocket. He would never ask me to pay for shit. That man spoiled me rotten.

"So, what's up with you?" She asked me. "I know it's got to be some shit if you here stealing all the bud." She shook her head. "Is it you and Trell?"

"Trell?"

"You need to stop frontin on Trell." She smiled. "You and that man got this connection or something. Y'all are like perfect for each other." She gave me a look and I had to stop myself from smiling. Brit could always see right through my bullshit.

"I mean—"

"Stop lying to yourself best friend, you love that man." She cut me off.

"Whoa." I started choking again. "I have feelings for Trell and things with us are okay, but he's the least of my problems."

"Problems?" She screwed up her face. "Ugh, is this about Shane?" The tone of her voice always let me know what she thought, and I could tell that she was so over Shane. Too bad, because I wasn't over him at all.

Brit started rolling her eyes. She got up and got two red party cups.

"You want some Henny?" she asked, looking through her cabinet. I could hear the liquor bottles clinking against each other and I knew that meant one thing; she was reaching for the big bottle of Henny. "Because I have a feeling that this whole conversation will need some Henny."

"You already know my answer to that, girl. I'm never going to turn down brown water. And don't give me no weak ass cup. I need that shit to have at least two or three shots."

"I know bitch."

She handed me the full cup. The smell hit me as I brought it to my lips. It made me smile and I knew that the high from the weed was kicking in. Now when this Henny mixed with it, it would make everything go even smoother. Fuck, I needed this after everything that was going on with Shane.

"You need to move on from this whole Shane thing. That nigga is nothing but drama now. Stay away from him and all that shit." Brit sipped from her cup shaking her head.

"Even him and that basic bitch?" I sat up.

"Yeah!" She gulped. "Let them run off and be two basic ass people together. You just got to let that shit go."

"How?" I really wanted to know. How was I supposed to let Shane go after everything we'd been through together?

"I don't know, but you can't keep living like this. You just got to take shit day by day. If you are always looking back at the bullshit, you'll never get ahead."

"What if I'm not ready to move on? What if I don't want to move on?"

"Didn't you tell me that Shane warned you to stay away?" She took another long gulp of the Henny and I did too.

"That bitch ass dude says a lot of things. One day we have a baby and he wanted to marry me. But now it's all different and he's all up on that ho."

"He's been with a lot of girls before."

"Yeah, but this one is different," I admitted.

I'd broken up other females from Shane and they all ran away screaming, but this bitch wasn't leaving so quick. She was sticking around, and Shane was being stupid enough to catch feelings for her. I couldn't believe he thought after everything we'd been through that I was just going to walk away. It was like he could look at all we had and think that it didn't mean anything. Who was this bitch? Why was he falling for her? Was he so stupid that he couldn't see that she was just some basic ugly bitch chasing a check? Where was she when he needed someone to hold him down? Where was she when he felt like nobody has his back? Who gave him his son? Who took care of his son? It was me! And he would throw all of that away over her? Fuck her.

"Well if she's different maybe it's really time to let it go." Brit said, and I shook my head. "Why not? You got Trell now, you don't need to be thinking about that nigga Shane. Let him cut you a check every month for the baby, and just move on. You not tired of the bullshit?"

"Brit, you have never been in love like I have," I told her straight up. "Me and Shane is something special, okay?" I sat up. "We have too much together for just one stupid ass bitch to stand in the way. Me, him, and our son are family. I'm not going to let him go."

Brit rolled her eyes again and I ignored it. She didn't know what I was going through, and she didn't know how it's like. When you have a love like me and Shane had, you got to hold on to it. You don't let nothing stand in the way. You have to hold on to it tight. I knew as soon as that bum bitch was out of the way, Shane would see that we are meant to be. He would remember all the good times we had and how I had his back. He was just letting this dumb bitch block us getting together. But you know what, I'd fix that soon.

"I can see that your brain is plotting some shit." Brit got up slowly. The weed and Henny must have been hitting her all at once. She started to almost fall on the way to the kitchen. She threw our cups in the garbage. "What you thinking about?"

"What you mean?" I leaned back and felt everything hit me too. Fuck, I loved riding this wave.

"Girl, bye. You already know that I know you. I can read your face and I know that you are up to some shit."

"Maybe." I smirked a little bit.

"I knew it." She plopped on her couch. "So, what are you going to do now? It's obvious that you're not going to give up on Shane."

"Don't worry about that." I laughed a little. I saw that she had a confused look on her face. "I got a plan Brit."

CHAPTER 2

Jayla

Every day wasn't such a good day, but damn, today was good. The sun was shining, the breeze was nice, and all the patients were being cool as hell. It was like everyone got on the same vibe today. Usually, we would all be dragging our ass waiting to clock out, but today, it was just a good day. I was so happy, I was damn near skipping down the hall and humming as I checked in with each patient.

"How are you Ms. Evans?" I sang as I walked in. "Do you need anything?" I asked. She looked over at me with sad eyes, but then she must have got hit by the vibe because she started smiling. She didn't answer me though, but just put her head back on her pillow. I stocked up her supplies, saw that someone had already cleaned and changed everything, so I turned on her TV. I knew she loved game shows, so I put one on with the volume on low. While I walked away, she reached out to squeeze my hand. Her eyes glowed and sparkled and I knew that was her way of saying 'thank you.' I simply gave her a smile, nodded, and went on my way.

Work was such an easy breezy today. When lunch time came around, I met my brother and his girlfriend at this local restaurant. It was a place that I wanted to try out badly, but it was always booked no matter the time. But today was the day of miracles because when I walked in, not only did we get a seat, but we got free appetizers because it was our first time. Damn today was such a good day.

"Good afternoon." I hugged my brother and his girl.

"You are such in a good mood," Crystal, Keon's girlfriend, said.

"Why shouldn't I be?" I asked. "Look at

this day." I pointed out the big glass windows.
"It's such a beautiful day." I sighed. They both looked out and slowly nodded.

"It's cool, but can you tone down the Mary Poppins act?" Keon joked and we all started laughing.

"So, tell me what' going on with you guys?"

The way they looked at each other and smiled, and it made me roll my eyes. They were so in love that it could be nauseating sometimes.

"Your brother is the perfect gentleman." Crystal smiled and used her finger to tap on his nose. "This morning he made me breakfast."

"He cooked?" I coughed.

"Yes, he did." She laughed.

"You know, I can cook." He started to defend himself.

"We know," Crystal and I said at the same time. Keon rarely cooked so it was like seeing a miracle right before our eyes.

"But here's the thing," Crystal went on. "I was the one who had to do the dishes."

"Hey! I cooked." He crossed his arms.

"You expect me to cook and do the dishes?" he joked.

"Whatever." She rolled her eyes at him. "I'm going to use the restroom real quick."

"Do you know what you want to eat?" I asked as she got up. "Or do you want us to wait for you to come back so that we all can order together?"

"Your brother knows what I want." She smiled, and he grinned right back at her.

When Crystal was out of sight, I started laughing.

"What's so funny sis?" He looked at me.

"You know what she wants?"

"I'm with her all the time," he told me. "Besides, she stays talking about this avocado thing, so I know that's what she wants." He smiled and then his face got nervous.

"What?"

"I got something to tell you, but I don't know how you gonna take it."

"Oh damn. What is it? She pregnant?"

"No!" He laughed. "Why was that the first thing you jump to?"

"Shit, the look on your face! I really thought that was it. What is it?"

"I'm going to propose to Crystal."

I was beyond shocked. I couldn't even move the first few seconds. I just had to keep staring at Keon. To see Keon now was amazing sometimes. I remembered all the trouble that he caused me. I remember thinking that I would be visiting him in jail or even worse. Now he had turned his life around for the better. He was almost done in school and now he was proposing to Crystal. Life can be crazy sometimes.

"Wow." I finally spoke.

"That's all you have to say?" He chuckled. His eyes were opened wide and his smile got even bigger. "I would have thought that you would be happy."

"Of course, I am happy!" I playfully hit him. "It's just that my brother is getting ready to get married. I can't believe it." I felt the tears well up in my eyes. I was so proud of him it hurt.

"Yeah there is something about Crystal that makes me want to keep her forever."

"I can see that you both really love each other."

"I love her, I really do." He looked down

at the menu, but there was no hiding how he felt. He didn't have to speak about how much he loved his girlfriend. It was so obvious.

"So, when are you going ring shopping? Do you know what you're going to get her? Do you know what style you're looking for? How much are you going to spend? How are you going to propose to her? Are you going to get her parents involved? Do you know when you're going to propose to her?"

"Damn Jayla." He sighed. "You ask all these questions like you a reporter or something.

"Well this is a very important time for you and for her. I just want it to be special."

"I know that. Look, I'm taking my time on this one, but I will let you in as much as I can. I just have to ask you to do one thing."

"What?"

"Don't tell her." He smiled. I gave him a look and stuck my tongue out at my brother.

While we ate lunch, it was so hard to look at Crystal knowing what I did. I wanted to tell her so badly because Crystal had become like one of my best friends. It was so crazy to think that soon we would be sisters. When I watched them together, I just felt so happy. Today was really a good day.

After work my day got even better because Shane surprised me by popping up at my job.

Usually I wasn't so crazy about people popping up on me, but it was nice seeing him.

"Well, what do we have here?" he joked, leaning on his car. "You can make that uniform look so sexy." He reached out to hug me.

"Oh yeah, you find dirty scrubs cute?" I asked. "Is it the stains or the ugly colors?"

"It's the person who is wearing them." He kissed my cheek and made me feel a way that only he could. Shane had this special thing about him. He could just touch you and you could feel your soul cry a little bit.

"What made you come here? I can drive myself home." I pointed towards my car.

"I know that. I was in the area scouting some places for new gyms and I thought I would stop by."

"Oh, that's nice."

"You're aren't happy to see me?" he asked, but he already knew my answer.

"I am happy to see you." I gave him my

biggest smile. "I've been having such a great day, and this made it even better."

A soft peck on the lips was supposed to be all that it was, but the next thing I knew, we were making out up against his car. He was grabbing me by my waist and my arms went around his neck. He leaned my neck back and gave me soft, wet, passionate kisses all over. I felt myself get horny and I had to snap out of it. I was still in front of my job, but it felt like we were in another zone.

"Okay, let's slow down," I said to him, but I was really talking to myself.

"Yeah, because this is not what I came for." He chuckled.

"And what is it you came for?" My eyebrows shot up.

"One, I had to see you, but I wanted to ask you out to dinner tonight."

"You could have sent that in a text." I gave him a look because he wasn't fooling anyone.

He licked his lips and smiled. I hated how much that man could turn me on within seconds.

"I like this way better." His smile was making me want to reach out and kiss him again, but I knew better than that. "So, may I please take you out tonight?"

"Of course."

We exchanged the details and I got in my car. My foot was pressed down on the gas and I was so glad that I didn't get pulled over. Last thing I needed was a ticket before this date. I just wanted to take a quick shower, change into something sexy, and go to dinner with Shane. Like always, I made sure I smelled good. I went straight to the rose scented bath options. As the shower ran, the smell filled up the room. When I finished, I put the raw shea butter on my face, and then put the rose scented lotion all over my body.

While I let the shea butter set, I went to my closet looking for an outfit. I didn't have to dig long when I pulled out this hot pink dress. It had one shoulder, short, and it hugged my body just right. I put it on the bed and dug in my dresser for some lacy underwear. After a while, I pulled out my white lace bra with matching lace boyshorts. I flat ironed my hair straight and put on makeup and matched my sexy dress with some red spiked heels. I was so ready to go.

It wasn't that long after when I heard a ring at my doorbell. I took one last look in the mirror and gave myself a wink.

"Damn," he said as soon as I opened the door.

"Is there something wrong?" I was playing stupid. I turned around, so he could get a good look at my dress. I wanted him to memorize my curves in this dress. When I turned back and looked at his face, I knew that I had him right where I wanted him.

"Shit." He moved back and took a deep breath. His eyes showed me how much he wanted me, and they were turning me on. "I'm trying not to get too excited, but damn baby." He tried to reach out to touch me, but I playfully hit his hand away. As much as I wanted him, I knew the second that he touched me...it was going to be over.

"We have a dinner to get to."

"I can eat something good right here." That damn naughty look in his eyes almost had me, but I had to be stronger.

"Let's go." I laughed and pushed him towards his car.

We got to the restaurant and it was just too

The lights were low, the music was tic, and the whole vibe was just great. He always picked the best places to go to. When the waiter came back with our drinks, I just looked around the room. It was a perfect place. Shane was such a gentleman, but his eyes kept wandering all over my body.

"Stay focused," I told him while I sipped my wine.

"How can I?" His eyes were filled with lust and I had to look away. "You wear something like that and you expect me to act like a saint?" He looked me up and down again. "You don't know the things I want to do to you, right here, right now." I was tempted to ask him for more details, but I wasn't trying to start anything in this restaurant. As much as he was talking about me, his well put together body looked so good in that blazer he was wearing. He paired it together with some dark jeans and it just made him look too good. I would sneak glances at other tables, and I could see the ladies looking at him too.

The whole date was good. We ate and after we finished, we went to a local spot. It was a bar, but there was a dance floor. I finally let Shane touch me. We danced slowly to the music and our bodies pressed against each other. He felt so good and it wasn't long before his hands slid down and grabbed my ass. I would have stopped him, but I didn't want to. His hands felt so good and when we kissed, I wanted him right there and then. My hands creeped down his chest. His muscles always turned me on. This man was so sexy, and it was getting harder not be all over him.

"You feel so good," he whispered in my ear. "How did I get so lucky?" He kissed my earlobe and then my neck. I felt my knees want to give in, but I just continued to dance. I swung around and pressed my ass against his crotch. I heard him grunt and when I turned my head around, I saw that his eyes were closed.

"You can't handle it?" I teased.

"You already know that I can." Seconds later I felt him poking me. "You want me to prove it to you?"

"How would you do it?" I dared him.

"Let me take you back to my place and show you."

"What's stopping you?"

Just like that we raced back to his car. Before we got in his car, he pulled me in, and kissed me. I fell in deeply and we started to make out against the car just like we did before. His hand slid down my ass and squeezed. I moaned out loud and bit his bottom lip. He slapped my ass lightly.

"You just don't know…" He didn't finish but his eyes said it all.

"Let's get in the car," I urged him.

"What if I told you that I can't wait?" His voice got deeper. His lips then pressed against my neck. He then bit my neck and I knew I was in trouble.

"You are not fucking me in your car. Nope, take me to your place." I tried to say it like I was demanding it, but really, I was begging him.

The car ride was quick. It seemed like we got to his house in seconds. As soon as we stepped in, our clothes went flying off. He grabbed me as I was in my bra and underwear.

"The second I saw you," he was saying to me, but I had a feeling he was talking to himself. His hands were firm on my ass, squeezing it hard. "I just want to..." He couldn't finish his sentences.

"What are you trying to say?"

"I think I'd better show you."

That's when he started get down on his knees. On his way down, he kissed my neck, my chest, and stomach. His tongue circled my belly button. He looked up and gave me a wink. I was about to ask him what he was doing, but then he pushed my panties to the side and pressed his lips against my lips. He kissed me softly and I sighed. His eyes were closed, and I could see that he was enjoying every part of this. His mouth was deep inside and his tongue had found a new warm home. It wasn't fair how he had me grabbing onto his shoulders, but when his tongue started moving in and out of me, all bets were off.

"Sssshaaane," I whispered stretching out his name because I felt like I was about to explode.

"Mmm-mm." He shook his head no and I damn near passed out. He wasn't going to let up. In fact, his tongue moved in and out of me faster. Then he had the nerve to pass his finger on my clit and from there, I zoned out.

All I remember was me throwing my body back against the wall as I tried to climb it at the same time. He took his arms and locked me in and I blacked out.

Somehow, we ended up in his bedroom. He opened my legs and slid one finger in slowly. I twisted a little because I was still trying to come back to life.

"It's so warm." I heard him mumble and by the time I brought my head up to see what he was doing, he was giving me mouth-to-lips again.

"Please." I barely spoke because I couldn't take it anymore. He kept licking, and tasting, and teasing me with his tongue. I couldn't even breathe and when he got on top of me and slowly went inside, I let out a small groan.

"You okay?" he asked but the look on his face showed that he was just so proud of himself. The nerve of him.

"It feels so good," I confessed, biting my lip.

"You the one that teased me by wearing that dress. I thought that this was the appropriate punishment." His voice was so smooth.

"You're punishing me with your tongue?" I asked and then he started stroking faster.

"Not just with my tongue." His grin was back. "I told you once I saw you in that dress that I was picturing all the things I wanted to do to you.'

"Oh my God." I wrapped my legs around his waist because I just had a feeling how the rest of the night was going to go.

"And like I told you earlier, I'm going to show you."

The night went on. He got on top of me, behind me, underneath me, to the side of me, Shane was everywhere. Just when I tapped out from one position, he had my legs going in another way. Then he would pull out and taste me again. What was he trying to do? Make me explode to death? I was gripping the sheets, biting down on the pillow, and screaming out for the saints. Shane was working me over. I never knew that sex could be too good that you would want to stop, just so that you could breathe. I just wanted to take a timeout, so I could have a sip of Moscato or a shot of something just so I could continue. I would have asked for a break too,

1ane was just so cocky that I couldn't let
'in. When I heard him chuckle as I
..ned into the pillow, I knew that playtime
was over.

I put him on his back and got on top. I
slid down slowly, clenched my muscles, and
started bouncing up and down. Leaning
forward and holding on to his muscular chest,
I threw my whole body against him. The
repetitive sounds of my body banging against
his made me smile. I put my whole effort into
it. Whirling my hips around, I saw that I had
him now. He was closing his eyes.

"Nah, you going to open your eyes now." I
squeezed my muscles.

"Shit," he cursed and then laughed a little.

"You think you the only one that can play
this game?" I asked and before he could even
answer I leaned back, grabbed his ankles, and
started hopping up and down.

"Fuck!" he screamed, and I kept going
until I felt him finish.

I got off him and fell hard against the bed.
All my strength was gone, but it was worth it.
Shane made me feel so good and it just wasn't
the sex. When I looked at him, I felt my heart

beat even faster. I hated to think that I was really falling in love with him because that was a scary place to be. There was that drama with his baby mama, but I hadn't had an issue ever since Shane put his foot down. If things continued to go on like this, who knew where this could go?

Pretty soon, I could hear that Shane was falling asleep. I moved up to him and placed my head against his chest. His heartbeat was still a little fast and I chuckled to myself. I took my fingers and traced a line around his lips before I planted a sweet kiss on it. To my surprise, Shane halfway opened his eyes and kissed me back.

"Goodnight," he mumbled.

"Goodnight."

CHAPTER 3

Jayla

The sound of the phone's alarm woke me up slightly, but I was still groggy that I could barely move. Sometime later, I heard some heavy footsteps around the room. Opening my eyes slowly, I saw that Shane was getting dressed. He had on a snug white tee, a black blazer, with matching black slacks. Even this early in the morning, Shane looked good. He leaned into the mirror while he brushed his hair. Every now and then he would look at his watch. I kept watching him until we locked eyes.

"How long have you been looking at me?" he asked, chuckling a little bit.

"Not for long." I yawned. I groaned and stretched out. Sitting up, my body still felt a bit sore from last night. "What time is it?"

"It's a little after 8:30." He looked at his watch. "I would stay here with you, but I'm meeting investors to talk about a possible expansion for one of the gyms." Shane was always busy. "You want me to drop you off at work?"

"I don't have to work today, but you can drop me off at home." I started to get ready. Looking around, I tried to remember where I put my clothes. On the corner of the bed, I spotted my clothes folded up. My bra was folded on top of my dress. I slid it on, but Shane stopped me from completely getting dressed.

"What are you doing?" he asked.

"Getting ready to go?"

"No, stay here," he said in a firm voice, but his eyes were begging. "If you don't have to go to work, you can stay here. I'll swing by later and we'll have brunch or something."

"Brunch?" I crossed my arms.

"You know, it's a combination of breakfast and lunch," he replied sarcastically.

"Shut up, Shane." I playfully hit him. "I know what brunch is." I rolled my eyes. "But why do you want me to stay here?"

"Oh, come on." He hugged and then he started to kiss my neck.

And just like that, I felt myself giving in. I really wanted to go home, take a shower, and just watch reality TV for a little bit. I even wanted to check in on Keon and see how he was doing with the whole engagement thing. There was so much I wanted to do, and here was Shane kissing on my neck and erasing all of that. He smelled so good and when his fingers touched the small of my back, the feeling spread all over my body. Shane had something that made me hooked. With one touch, I was suddenly addicted to him. His hands started to travel down my body. He squeezed my ass softly and then nice and hard.

"What are you doing?" I whispered, but I wasn't talking to him. I was talking to me! Jayla, what are you doing falling for this guy this hard? I kept asking myself, but with his tongue on my neck and his hands all over my body, it was hard to listen myself.

"If I didn't have this meeting." He let go of me slowly and I could still smell him on me.

"But stay here and I'll order breakfast for you."

"You don't have to do that." But he already had his phone out.

"Now back into bed." He handed me his shirt and a pair of boxers.

"This better be clean." I gave it a careful sniff and he laughed.

"It's new." He held up an empty bag. "Just catch some sleep." He started to walk away but then he stopped.

"What is it?"

"The remote is on the nightstand." He gave me a knowing grin.

"What?"

"I already know." We both laughed. "You got to catch up on your shows."

"Well, no."

"Sure." He smiled.

"Not right now, at least."

I stretched and leaned back into bed. He came over and threw the blankets over me.

Then he started to stuff them under me, tight.

"Hey!" I laughed. "What are you doing?"

"I'm making sure that you stay here," he joked. "I'm going to come back later and unwrap you for brunch." He winked and then kissed my forehead. "The food should be coming soon." He started walking towards the door.

The front door slammed, and I thought about watching TV, but decided against it. One, Shane really did tuck me in tightly, and two, I really wanted to catch up on some more sleep. All the sex from last night really made me restless this morning. I snuggled some more and loosened up the grip that the sheets had on me. Turning over on to my stomach, I felt myself get a little sleepy. I couldn't sleep too much though because I had to stay awake for the food, but knowing Shane, he'd probably figure out some way I could get it anyway.

I was about to fall asleep when I heard the front door close again. Shane just couldn't get enough of me. I knew when he touched my body that he wasn't going wait to until brunch.

His investors would just have to see him another time, because Shane wanted morning sex.

The footsteps got closer to the bedroom and when they were just a few steps away, alarm bells went off in me. I was still groggy, but I was sure I heard something else.

"I said 'wake the fuck up!" this voice urged, and I slowly got up. I opened my eyes and my mouth dropped. "Are you surprised, bitch?"

"Damiah, what are you-" I stopped speaking once I saw she had a gun in her hand. "What..." I started to speak again but my mouth got dry.

CHAPTER 4

Shane

Walking into the gym, everything seemed to be running in order. This new branch was making more money than we expected. With the college students always coming in, the new hospital being built down the street, and the condos rising all over this neighborhood, we didn't really think we would be flooded like this. This was why we needed to purchase the property that was right next door. It was a two-floor building with an empty lot next to it. We planned to make a second mini gym and turn the empty lot into a parking lot. That was why we needed to talk to the investors; we needed more money, and as soon as they saw how busy we are, they would know they would get their money back easily.

The meeting went great, but I couldn't take my mind off Jayla. It was that damn dress that she wore last night that really made me go crazy. It just fit her body right and she knew it too. As soon as she opened the door, my eyes were stuck all over her body. Had she let me, I would have taken her down right there and then. It was so hard during dinner to not touch her. And when I say it was hard, I really do mean "it." I had to keep my cool, but the second I touched her, I couldn't hold back anymore. We went at it almost all night. She felt so good and soft. She had this playful look in her eyes, and it made me just go crazier.

"Sir?" One of the investors' voice shook me out of my daydream.

"I'm sorry. I was just crunching some figures," I lied.

"That's why I like working with you, Shane." The other investors started smiling.

"You're always making sure that the money is right." He reached out to shake my hand. "I don't need to hear anything else. I hope I speak for the rest of us, but we're ready to go. Send the paperwork over and the money we'll be sent right away."

"That's great because we have the real estate agent ready with the owners of the property," I informed them.

"Let's get it started." He replied.

The meeting ended, and I looked down at my phone. I saw a text message from the diner where I ordered Jayla's breakfast. It read that nobody was home, so the food was brought back to the restaurant. Maybe she overslept and didn't hear the people at the door. I looked at the text message that I sent to Jayla during the beginning of the meeting. When one of the investors were running late, I cancelled brunch but told her that I would come see her after work. She didn't send anything back, which was weird because she always made sure to reply to my messages.

I called her, and the rings slowly went to voicemail.

"Hey, the restaurant sent me a text message saying that you didn't open the door for breakfast. I guess you were very tired. Did you get my text letting you know that I won't make it to brunch? I'm going to see you right after work." I ended the call.

"Who was that?" My right-hand man, Tone walked in.

"Nobody." I sighed. "Just calling Jayla."

"Ooh," he teased. "You still stuck on Jayla?"

"Don't start." I rolled my eyes. Tone was never about settling down with chicks. He loved the fact that being successful meant that he could have as many ladies as he wanted.

"I'm just playing with you. I know you got feelings for that girl."

"I do. She's not like any woman that I met."

"I can see that. The other females you dealt with, you would have left them by now. She's got to be something special for you to be on her like that."

"She is. And last night, she finally spent the night over."

"Oh, for real."

"Yeah, she's at my house right now."

The thought of Jayla at my house made me smile a little. Tone shook his head.

"You really feeling her, huh?" He laughed.

"I am just glad that she finally stayed over the night at my house. I'm not going to lie, I'm kind of excited to go home and see her there."

"Excited? You're excited?"

"Yeah, I am. Is that a problem?"

"You sound like a little kid! You're a man!" He patted me on my back.

"I know that, but I'm happy that she's at the crib." I laughed. "Damn, can't I be happy about that?"

"Yeah, but you got me here feeling like I'm in middle school or something," Tone joked.

"I'm serious though, I was even thinking about something."

"What is that?"

"I want her to meet my son."

"Oh shit."

Tone knew just like I knew about crazy Damiah, but I didn't want to keep my son and Jayla apart anymore. I know for a fact that Jayla is going to be a big part of my life. And if I felt that she was going to be a big part of my life, that meant she had to meet my son.

Now, I knew that Damiah wasn't going to like it, but she was going to have to get over it, because I was going to try my best to make it happen.

"I don't know about that, man." Tone sighed. "You know how your baby mama is." He shook his head. "She crazy as fuck and you know that."

"I know but-"

"But what? She already tried some shit with Jayla and that is before Jayla has met your son. What do you think she's going to do if she finds out you're going to try to introduce your son to Jayla? She's going to go even crazier." He wiped his hand across his forehead. "Look, I know that you're feeling Jayla and she's great, but slow down. You got your businesses to think about and you have to make sure that this situation with Damiah is really under control."

Tone was making a lot of sense. I knew that I should slow it down with Jayla, but it wasn't easy. After spending all that time with her last night, I knew that her meeting my son was naturally the next step. But until I could say for sure I had a hold on Damiah, I was going to slow down. I needed her to be calm. The last thing I needed is to get Damiah upset. Who knew what she might do?"

CHAPTER 5

Damiah

I was trying not to laugh, I really was, but this thot ass bitch wasn't making it easy. She woke up and look like she was about to piss all over the sheets. Her eyes were open wide, and she was shaking.

"Damiah?" She was whispering, and her voice shook. I held back a laugh.

"I warned you, didn't I? I told you to stay away from Shane, didn't I? So, did you think I was playing?" I was screaming and then I pushed the gun to her temple. "Now you see that I'm not bullshitting?" I grinned.

"What?"

"Is that all you have to say?"

I was getting angrier. Just looking at this simple bitch in Shane's bed pissed me off.

That's when I noticed something. She was wearing Shane's shirt. I pulled the sheets from her and saw that she was wearing his boxers. This bitch was really trying to put herself in my life. She was in my man's bed, wearing my man's clothes, and trying to steal my man away.

The first time I smacked her with the gun, I didn't mean to. I just snapped looking at her trying to be like me. I can still remember waking up in Shane's bed after we spent all night fucking. I would just chill in bed and he'd go find some way to make money. Now he was just going to do that with this basic ass bitch? That thought just pissed me off and the next thing I knew, I smacked her across the face with the gun. After the first time, I smacked her again and again.

"You stupid, worthless bitch!" I yelled as I kept hitting her. "Stop trying to live my life! You can't have this life! This my fucking life!" I yelled, and she kept howling in pain. Even when she was crying and begging for me to stop, it did nothing but piss me off more. Why should I stop? She was the one that brought this to herself. I did the bitch a favor by even warning her. She was lucky that I didn't run up on her with the strap right in front of her fucking job.

The bitch fell to the floor.

"Dummy." I kicked her a little bit and she barely moved. Now she was just acting like she was really hurt, but I knew better. She just wanted me to feel bad for her because she thought it was going to make me stop, but she was wrong. Once I got started, I was not going to stop at all. The room got really quiet and that was when I noticed that the little bitch passed out. So, on top of her trying to steal my life and basically be me, she was a little pussy too. Un-fucking-believable.

She started groaning so I figured that she decided to wake up.

"Had a nice little nap?" I laughed. "You're so pathetic." I kicked her, and I heard her groan. She was trying to say something, but I guess the bitch was in pain because all I heard was her whimper. "That's right thot. You should know your place is beneath me." I laughed and reached into my back pockets. I got some zip ties out. She was still barely moving so I tied up her arms together and then tied up her feet.

She finally started to really move. Her eyes started opening slowly. When she looked up and saw me she tried to move, but then she must have realized that she was tied up.

"Oh my God!" she screamed. "Let me go!"

"I'm not doing that shit." I laughed. "Why would you even waste your time by even asking me?"

"Help! Somebody help me!" She started yelling and tried to break out of the zip ties, but I tied them tight, so I knew she wasn't going anywhere.

"You're wasting your time," I told her.

"Help!"

"Be quiet." I yawned, but she got even louder, and I didn't want the chance that someone could hear her and call the police. I took out my gun and pressed it against her temple. "Be fucking quiet!" I screamed, and she started crying. "You making all this noise. It's like you forgot that this is all your fault. I told you to stay away from my man and you didn't listen. This is what you get." I started to look around the house. "This is my life. This is my house."

The bitch got quiet because she knew what I could do. I pushed the gun to her head even more just so I could see how afraid she was. The tears were streaming down her face and she was crying quietly. What did Shane see in this bitch? Look at how ugly she looked right now.

"Please," she whispered but I shook my head and then tapped the gun on her nose softly.

"No more talking. It's time for you to go to the closet while I go get some things from my house." She started to nod her head and I smiled. "That's right."

I bent over and grabbed her hair and started pulling her towards the closet. She started screaming in pain, so I took the gun back out. "Now come one, I thought we had an agreement." I pushed the gun against her forehead. "You be quiet while I get some things." I squatted down so that I could look her dead in the eyes. "Are we going to play nice now?" She nodded her head. "You're not as dumb as I thought." I took the gun away slowly. "Now be quiet." I pulled hard and she grunted, but she didn't scream. I flung her body in the closet and then closed the door. "Now where is the money stash?"

CHAPTER 6

Shane

"What can I get for you sir?" I was up at the counter ready to get some nice halal food. I'd been thinking about Jayla all day and it wasn't until my stomach started growling that I realized that I needed to eat. I was calling her and sending her text messages, but she still didn't reply. Everything was going to voicemail. I guess she was busy.

"Let me just get a chicken gyro, chicken and rice, and some lamb and rice," I ordered.

"Well damn, are you going to eat all that food by yourself?" Tone asked laughing.

"I ordered some for you too. You always order the lamb and rice."

"It's the best." He smiled. "I'm starving. After you finished kissing up to the investors, I had to get all the paperwork ready so that we could get started. Then I got to the real estate agent to give them a tour of the possible property next door."

"What did they think about it?"

"They love it. They can't wait to get started. I called the contracting company, so everything is in place."

"That's great."

We finished eating our lunch with Tone telling me about the new woman he was dealing with. She was a middle school teacher and she had a crazy body. Crazy enough, he met her in the strip club.

"That's wild." I shook my head as we got back to work.

"What? What is it you're trying to say? You're trying to say that middle school English teachers can't have fun?"

"I'm not saying that at all. I'm just trying to picture a middle school teacher up in the strip club."

"Well what did you think she was doing? Did you think she was there grading papers and handing out homework?" We both started laughing.

"You stupid. So, does that mean you're settling down?"

"She's a teacher...not a miracle worker."

I tried to get back to work, but for some reason, I couldn't get Jayla out of my head. I kept looking at my phone waiting to see if I got a text message from her, but there was nothing. Maybe she was busy, but that feeling in my gut wouldn't leave me. I took out my phone and called again, but like all the other times, she didn't pick up and now the voice-mail was full.

"What's going on?" Tone asked as he knocked on my office door. I saw he had some files in his hand. He put them on my desk and sat on the chair opposite of me. He leaned back and when I didn't answer him, his face got serious.

"What?"

"Why didn't you answer my question?" He screwed up his face and crossed his arms. "I know you heard me."

"I did."

"Then, what's up?"

"I just didn't want to hear your mouth if I brought up Jayla again."

"Damn, I was only joking with you. I know you really feeling her and that's cool. What's up? Why you look so stressed?"

Tone's face was full of concerned and I finally told him.

"Man, I've been trying to reach Jayla all day and she hasn't replied to me once."

"Okay?" He shrugged his shoulders. "I still don't get why you look so mad? Maybe she's busy with something and she can't get to the phone."

"That's what I thought at first too, but I know Jayla. If Jayla is busy, she always sends me a text message letting me know what's up."

"She probably is really busy. If she's always hitting you back, all you have to do is wait."

"I am waiting, but I don't know, I just got this weird feeling."

I turned back in the chair and looked out at the gym. The customers were using the machines, eating at the small cafe, drinking from the juice bar, and all having a good time. I was basically making a lot of money right now, but my mind was somewhere else. This feeling in my gut was driving me crazy.

"Don't stress it too much," Tone said out of nowhere. He must have read my face when I turned back around. "If she's a good girl, you have nothing to worry about."

"I'm not thinking she's out there with some other dude." I quickly brushed that off. "I have no worries in that department."

"Then, what is it?"

"Just this feeling in the pit of my stom-ach." I closed my eyes. "I think I might have to leave work early."

"What?" Tone reached for the papers he just put on my desk. "If you'd bother to read these, you'd know that I need you to sign these before the work day ends. You need to go over them."

"Listen Tone, I hear what you're saying, but something is not right."

"What if her phone just died? You'll be going crazy over nothing."

"That would make sense except for the fact that her phone keeps ringing and then going to voicemail. If it was dead, it would be going straight to voicemail."

"What if she's ignoring you? What if she wants some space?"

"Then that's something I need to go and find out."

Tone's face had some concern and I couldn't tell if it was for Jayla or for the papers he needed me to go over.

"Look, I'll read this as quickly as I can, but at the end of the day, I trust you. I know you can take care of this and your signature on this is just as good as mine." I stood up. "But I really got to go and take care of this." I got up and started walking to my office door.

"I'm not going to stop you." He got up and patted me on the back. "If you need any help, you know where to find me."

"I do." I grabbed my jacket.

"I hope you're wrong and she's just ignoring you." His voice started to fade away as I started walking to the exit.

"I hope so too."

CHAPTER 7

Damiah

Finding his stash wasn't easy, but I knew
Shane too well. He had a fake safe and when
I finally cracked it open, it had nothing but
paperwork for his gyms. Shane thought he
was slick, but when I looked in his closet, I
found his stash. He put it in some shoeboxes
and after throwing them all around, I found it.
 Then I found some jewelry and put it all in
garbage bags. I started stacking them the front
door.

"Now, to finish this all."

I went into his bathroom and got some of
his colognes out. I poured them out and got

some alcohol and poured it all over the bathroom and the living room. Looking through some of the stuff in his house, I just wanted to read one phrase before I opened it. "Extremely flammable." Once I read those words, I opened it up and poured it all over the house. I found some lighter fluid outside next to his grill. This was perfect. I was going to burn this house down to teach Shane a lesson. Not only would he lose his house, but that dumb thot ass bitch would be gone too. Killing two birds with one stone.

Suddenly I heard a scream. I guess that bitch was breaking our agreement. When I opened the closet, she was still screaming but now it was louder. I pulled her by her hair and dragged her out.

"Dumb bitch." I kicked her, and she yelled. "You think this is a game?" I knelt next to her. "I've poured alcohol all over this house and I'm going to burn it down to flames." She screamed louder. I took the gun and smacked her again. "Shut the fuck up, stupid! I warned you about this shit. I fucking warned you and now you're going to pay. Now you're going to pay for trying to take over my life and taking my man. Did you think that I was going to go away? Did you think that I was going to just leave and let you skip off into the sunset with my baby daddy? You stupid thot. Now you know the truth."

She started to scream again, and I slapped her one more time. Just when I was about to hit her one more time, there was a noise at the door. My stomach started doing flips. I looked at the time and knew that Shane was supposed to be still at work. The chick must have heard the noise too because she started screaming. I pointed the gun right in her face. She got really quiet.

"You make another sound and it will be your last one, do you hear me? I will end your life right here and right now."

The front door slammed, and I could hear the footsteps coming towards the bedroom.

"Fuck!" I whispered. I picked her up and started bringing her back in the closet. Out of nowhere, she screamed,

"Somebody helped me!" Before she could get any louder, I covered her mouth with my hand. I put the gun against her temple.

"Say bye-bye." I grinned, and she shook her head no. "Are you going to be quiet now?" She nodded her head. "You should be because I've been giving you one too many chances. Now you're going to stay in this closet and shut the fuck up. Do you fucking understand me?" I asked her, and she nodded her head again. "Now, I'm going to remove my hand from your mouth. If you make a sound, a bullet will rip through that pretty head of yours before you can finish the word." I tapped the gun against her head softly. "And you've run out of chances."

I made sure I closed the closet door softly. I didn't know what was going to happen, but I was not going to go out like no punk. If me and Shane were going to fight, I'd be ready for him. Before he could even think about saving his bitch, I might have to teach him a lesson too. I might have to teach him about how to treat me and how to leave that thot in his past.

The footsteps were going through the whole house. One second, they were getting closer to the room and the next, I could have sworn I heard them going in the kitchen. What the fuck is going on? I tiptoed out of this bedroom and held the gun close to my side. I put my finger on the trigger, ready for anything that could happen. I didn't come this far to turn back around and leave. I'd done too much to turn back now. The footsteps got louder and the next thing I knew they were right behind me. I closed my eyes, held a tight grip on my gun, and turned around.

"What the fuck are you doing here, Trell?"

CHAPTER 8

Trell

To say that I was surprised seeing Damiah would be saying the least. Seeing her with a gun in her hand shocked the shit out of me. She was the last person I expected to see in Shane's house. But Damiah was always stuck on Shane, so maybe I should have expected to see her just a little bit. But I wasn't expecting none of this at all.

Just a few hours ago, I was sitting in the crib drinking some Bacardi and orange juice. I was feeling uptight and the drink was supposed to make me chill. Shane and his bullshit had been on my mind and the more I thought about it, the more pissed off I got. That's why I settled on just drinking. It was all going good until I went out to get my mail. When I looked through the bills and all the bullshit letters, I saw Shane's smile. It was a flyer saying that he was opening another gym.

That picture of Shane got me tight. There was nothing that Bacardi or even Hennessy could do to bring me down. Fucking Shane was trying to rub it in my face with his money. If it wasn't for me, he wouldn't have none of this success. I fucking made that nigga and he had the nerve not to pay his dues. Did he ever come around and thank me for all I've done? No! Of course not. All he did was act like he built it himself, forgetting who made him and who got him there. Sitting at home and sipping while looking at his goofy ass just kept making me angry. It wasn't doing me no good, so I came over to Shane's house to claim what was mine. But Damiah standing here with a gun was not the welcome I was planning to see.

"What are you doing here Trell?" Damiah asked again, looking me right in the eyes. Why she had to be fine and looking as good as she did? Even with the gun in her hand, she was still hands down the prettiest chick I ever saw. Shane was dumb for even thinking of letting this one go. How could he live with himself making a dumb ass decision like that? On top of being shady in business, he was a fool at life.

"I could ask you the same question." I smirked looking up and down her body. The gun in her hand meant business, but her body was all play. With that all black outfit on, I could still see her curves. That ass was calling out to me, but I was still curious to know why she was here. "And why are you here with a gun?" I added that question on top.

"I don't even want to say." She smiled a little bit and shook her head. "It's been a crazy day."

"Come on, you know you can tell me anything." I playfully held her face. Her soft lips looked so juicy that I had to stop myself from leaning in and kissing her. I still had to play it cool. "So, tell me what's going on."

"I came here…" She stopped herself and then looked down at her feet. She then stared at the gun in her hand. "I came here to take care of business." Her voice was tough, and I knew she meant what she said.

"What do you mean by business?"

"I'm here to take care of that bitch that is fucking Shane."

Shane had always been her drug or weakness. Damiah didn't think straight if it was about Shane. She was all or nothing when it has to do with Shane. I know if Shane was out of the way, she would give me and her a real chance, but if Shane was around, she was going to follow him like a puppy.

"So why are you here?" She crossed her arms and looked at me.

"I'm here to take care of Shane," I told her firmly.

There was a flash of sadness in her eyes. It was that addiction of her showing itself again. There was a part of her that would always feel for Shane and that made sense. Shane and Damiah were with each other for a long time and they had a kid. Shit like that gets under your skin and lives there, but I knew Shane was not the man for Damiah. Shit, Shane was barely a man at that. He was more like a grown ass boy trying to be a man and Damiah couldn't really see it. She fell for Shane at a young age and it was hard for her to let go, but it wouldn't be too long. Shane was fucking up by trying to move on, and we both knew that.

"I see." She nodded her head softly. Her eyes kept racing around the house. I followed, and I saw what she was looking at. I took a deep sniff into the air and smelled all the scents. It was a lot going on, so I went to the windows and opened them a little bit.

"What's that smell?"

"Alcohol, gasoline, and some other stuff." She gave me a little smile.

"You were going to set this place on fire?" My eyes opened wide. She gave me a nod and I laughed. "Well you are about your business."

Then I heard a little noise from the bedroom. "What's that?" I questioned looking towards the room. "You brought someone with you?"

"No, I got that bitch in the closet." She smiled, and I smiled right back.

"Yo, you really about that life." I held her face. "I don't know what Shane is doing."

"What do you mean?" she asked but I knew she knew what I was talking about.

"You're special Damiah. You're the type of ride-or-die chick guys want. Shane is a dumbass if he doesn't see it. You're like the perfect package, baby. You're pretty, smart, and about your business. You making money at the salon and you still looking like this." I spun her around and took a good look at her whole body. "Shane is fucking stupid for leaving you. I would never do that."

"Never?" Her lips got closer to mine. We were centimeters apart and I finally replied,

"Never."

We kissed. The next thing I know we were walking to the bedroom kissing. I started to take off her clothes, and she put her gun down so she could take off mine. We got to the bed and my lips were all over her neck. Kissing her body, licking her, and she started to moan. I knew she was getting wet between the legs and I wanted all of that to be mine. She grabbed me by the back of my head and kissed me hard. Her body all up on me felt so right.

"Damn, I want you baby," she whispered in my ear.

"You already know how I feel about you," I told her while I was kissing her.

"Should have been with you instead of Shane," she told me when she laid on top of the bed. She opened her legs and slid her hand right over her pussy. She began playing with her clit and that got my dick rock hard. She circled her hand right around the top and I could hear how wet she was getting. I stuck my finger in her mouth and then took it out and slid it inside her. She giggled as I touched her, and I felt her walls get a tight grip on my finger.

"You want this D?" She nodded her head to this question. I pulled my dick out my boxers and came over her body.

Usually at a moment like this, I would slide into her quickly, but the way it was going, I was going to take my time. Damiah was that type of chick that made you want to take advantage of every second you had with her. You couldn't just fuck her quick, nut, and then get off of her. Nah, you had to hit her at every spot, so that's what I did. When I went deep, I bit her shoulders and her neck, so she could feel every inch of me. I held myself there and she shook her body beneath me.

"Take it," I told her.

"You already know I can handle you Zaddy, so why are you holding back?" So, I didn't.

Just then there was a kick in the front door.

I could hear more than one person running in.

"Oh fuck!" Me and Damiah said. We both scrambled to get dressed. She went to get the gun and we both waited.

"Jayla!" Shane was yelling, and I heard other people with him. Before I could reach for my strap, there was a bunch of niggas in the room with us.

"What the fuck?" One of them said. There was a lot of them and I didn't know all of them. Of course, there was bitch ass Shane, but when I saw Tone I got angry. He was a traitor just like Shane. I should have known that both of them turned on me. I wouldn't be surprised if they were always working together behind my back.

"Where is Jayla?" Shane asked and Damiah immediately sucked her teeth right after.

"Who cares?" She rolled her eyes.

"The fuck are both of you doing here?"

"I came to get what's mine." I reached to grab my gun, but before I pulled it out, Shane ran up and tackled me. He got me on the floor and threw a punch on my face. He didn't get to really hit me because I moved a little bit. He tried to choke me, but I pushed him off me. I tried to reach for my gun again, but bitch ass Tone kicked it away from me.

"Motherfucker." Tone kicked me and then I grabbed his leg before he could kick me again. That's when his boys jumped in.

"Fuck you!" Damiah screamed, pointing the gun at one of the boys, back but Shane pushed her. The gun went off and pieces of the ceiling fell. His boys went to wipe their faces and I took the chance to stand up. I started fighting one of the boys while they were trying to get the dirt out of their eyes. In the background, some chick was screaming at the top of her lungs. I was guessing it was that Jayla chick I kept hearing about. Shane pushed Damiah, trying to get to the closest, and that pissed me off.

"That's the mother of your son, bitch!" I yelled and jumped on Shane. His boys kept trying to jump in but Damiah put her gun up.

"Stay back bitches." She laughed. "This bitch ass nigga is getting what he deserves." She turned her head and looked at me. "Beat his ass." I punched him across the face and that shit connected. Then I hit him twice in the ribs and that bitch groaned. Finally, after all this time, I had my hands-on Shane. I was going to make him pay for everything.

Before I could really hurt him, Tone reached for Damiah and she shot another one in the air. I turned just a little bit and that bitch took that chance to push me. He reached down to the floor and grabbed my gun. He pointed it in my face and had his hand on the trigger. Damiah pointed her gun at him.

"Damiah...put the gun down," Shane told her, but she didn't move.

"You fucking put the gun down. All this over that basic bitch?" I could hear that she wanted to cry, but her face was strong. "I'm gonna get rid of that bitch. I warned you that I would."

"You do that, and my son will have no mother."

When he said that Damiah screamed and ran up on him. Tone grabbed her, and the gun let out another shot. She snatched herself away and that was when I yelled at her that we had to go.

"I'll fuck her up again, Shane!" Damiah yelled while we ran away. "There is nowhere that bitch can go where I won't find her! I'll get her Shane! Fuck that basic bitch!" And we were out.

~

Jayla

HEARING the gun shots had me shook. I was rocking back and forth in the closet. I wanted to keep screaming, but I was afraid that Damiah would turn the gun to the closet and just start shooting. I heard more fighting and then heard Damiah screaming about me. Finally, there was a sound at the closet door.

"Oh Damiah." Shane sighed. He had sadness all over his eyes and when he reached out for me, I flinched. I was still so scared. I didn't know why, but I thought that Damiah was going to pop up again.

"Is she gone?" I knew I was scared but it

wasn't until I heard how my voice shook that I knew I was really scared.

"She's gone," he let me know, and he started to untie me. My arms felt weak and my feet were numb. I felt woozy and when I looked up at Shane, I saw he had tears in his eyes. Next thing I knew, I passed out.

The beep of the machines woke me up. I didn't have to open my eyes to know that I was in a hospital. I'd been a CNA long enough to know the sounds of a hospital by heart. I slowly opened my eyes and saw that I was lying in bed. I looked in the corner and saw Keon and Crystal sitting together, and on the other side of the room, Shane was standing alone. I opened my mouth to speak, but then I felt something on my face. I took my hands and felt bandages on my face. I should have known that when Damiah beat on me, that she did damage.

"Jayla?" Crystal was the first person by my side. "I'm so sorry." She started crying and I teared up too. To think that this morning the only thing I was thinking of was how Keon was going to propose to her, and now I was here. I looked back at Shane and for a quick second, I saw Darius. It was like I was holding his bleeding body all over again. I could have died, and I would have seen Darius for real.

"Are you okay?" Shane said when he saw that I was looking at him. I couldn't speak to him. Everything that happened was because I was involved with him. If I'd let Shane alone, Damiah would have never got to me. I wouldn't be in the hospital right now if I didn't mess with Shane. My life would be so much better. "Jayla?" He started walking towards me and my heart started to beat quickly.

"Are you okay Jayla? You're crying," Crystal pointed out. I felt my cheeks and tears were rolling down my face.

It wasn't that long before I started really crying. Just the memories of what just happened, and the memories of Darius made me really start bawling. Looking at Keon and Crystal, thinking of my little sister in college, I knew that I didn't want to leave them behind. I could have been in a morgue instead of in a hospital bed. All of this for what? All this trouble for Shane. It wasn't worth it.

"Jayla?" Shane was next to me now, but

when he reached for me, I moved back again. My heart started racing and the machine that read my heartbeat sped up too. It was so fast, and I started shaking. "Jayla?" He reached again, and I shook my head no, with more tears running down my face.

"Please leave," I whispered so low that I barely heard myself.

"What is that?" Crystal asked and leaned in, so she could hear me. "What did you say?"

"Please tell him to leave." I looked right at her because I felt safe around Crystal. She looked in my eyes and I saw how loving they were. She nodded slowly.

"I think you should go." She stood up and crossed her arms. She was being so strong, and I felt a bit happier. In the corner, Keon sat there holding his head. Even though he wasn't speaking, I knew he was going crazy in his mind. He knew how much drama I went through with Darius. I could feel his anger from here.

After Crystal told Shane to leave, he didn't fight it. He just looked at me and his eyes were begging me to change my mind. But no matter how he sorry I knew he was, I just couldn't do it. I kept seeing him and Darius together. Both put me in so much trouble and both I fell for. I was done with that shit.

"Please," he kind of begged me. His words and body language told me he was sorry, but I was done. I was in a fucking hospital room all because of him. What was I going to wait for? Was I going to wait for Damiah to really kill me?

"She already said you have to go." Keon finally spoke in a low voice. The whole room's vibe changed. He was holding back his anger and I knew it. Shane nodded his head slowly. He knew that we weren't changing our minds on it.

"I understand." He was speaking to Keon, but then he turned to me. "I'm sorry Jayla. You know how I feel about you and you know I didn't want this for you at all. I should have handled Damiah better." He stopped speaking but I knew he wasn't done. "Whenever you are ready to talk to me, I'm here for you."

After he left, the whole room got quiet.

Keon walked over to me slowly. His face looked so hard, but his eyes were soft.

"I'm so sorry sis." He held my hand and squeezed it.

"You know...," I said to him. He looked confused, so I spoke a little more. I knew if I said this one thing, he would get where I'm coming from. "Darius."

"I get it." He shook his head. He was so angry, and it made sense, but I was afraid of that. I didn't want him to go back to his old ways just to protect me. I liked the good path that he was on. He was almost done with school and he was headed to career. I didn't want the drama that I was in to change his life for the worse.

Before I could tell him that, there was a knock at the door. A nurse walked in with two guys in suits. They didn't have to introduce themselves because I just knew they were the police.

"How you're doing?" one of them asked. When I saw his eyes, I knew my injuries were kind of bad because he could barely look at me.

"I'm okay," I lied. "I've had better days." I tried to joke but it didn't feel real.

"If you don't mind, we'd like to ask you a few questions about what happened today."

I took in a deep breath because I knew I would need every piece of strength to go through this story.

"I was staying at my—" I cut myself off. How was I going to describe Shane? Was I supposed to tell these cops that I was fucking with Shane? "I was at this guy's house and while I was sleeping, Damiah broke in." I was sobbing now. "She put a gun to my head. She started to beat me up, tie me up, dragged me in the closet, and all this other shit." I broke down and started sobbing hard.

"Take your time," one of the detectives said.

"She was going to kill me. She was planning to burn the house down with me in it." I cried out and I saw Crystal walk out the room.

"How do you know this?" the other detective asked.

"Because she poured out alcohol everywhere and told me. She would have done it but there was a knock at the door. She put me back in the closet and I heard her say 'Trell.'"

"Do you know this Trell person? Did you get a look at him?"

"No, but I did hear his voice."

"That's good. "

The two detectives looked at each other and kept writing down all the details that I could give them. It hurt to even think about what happened, but I didn't want Damiah to come after me. After Darius was killed, I just knew that his wife had something to do with it.

Besides the nightmares of the night he died, I just kept thinking what if his wife came after me. The police never arrested her and now I had a crazier female to deal with. Damiah wanted to get at me and I had to do all that I can to make sure that she was gone.

The detectives left and as soon as they were gone, Keon was up. He started pacing the room.

"Are you okay?" I asked him, and he stopped short. He huffed around, and I knew he was pissed.

"Am I okay? What about you? Are you okay? Jayla!" He shouted.

"Ssh." I shushed him. "I don't need these detectives coming back for you."

"But Jayla…" He stood right next to me. He held my hand and looked at me. "What would I have done if…" He didn't finish saying the sentence and he didn't have to. It was the same thought that was running through my head while I was in the closet.

"But I'm here." I tried to give him my best smile. "That's why I told the police every-thing, because I want them to handle it." I gave him a knowing look, but I couldn't read his face. I really didn't want Keon to get back into the street life.

Keon and Crystal went home, and I was left alone with my thoughts. I tried not to think about Shane, but I couldn't help it. I really was falling for Shane. No scratch that, I was in love with him, but I loved my safety more. Loving Shane was not worth all this drama. I was about to meet Jesus over a rela-tionship with Shane.

I should have left Shane alone when he didn't tell me about his kid and baby mama. That was the first red flag, but I was attracted to him and he made me feel great, so I stuck around. Then Damiah popped up at my job and Shane managed to keep me near after that. There were so many signs that the drama was just getting worse and I still stayed around.

Darius' death should have warned me against Shane. It was like as soon as the night-mares stopped, I stupidly let my guard down. I loved Shane, but I could not live my life like this. I could not sacrifice my life for him. I had a family to think about. Just looking at Crystal's and Keon's reaction, I didn't even want my little sister to hear about this. She was doing so good in college that the last thing I needed for her was to flunk out worrying about me. I refused to live my life in danger. I was done with Shane.

CHAPTER 9

Jayla

It had been a couple of weeks since the whole situation with Damiah and I hadn't really left the house. I'd been to the check the mail, the grocery store once, and then to the precinct because the police had more questions. I hadn't been to work at all, and luckily for me, I had so many sick days and vacation days that I really didn't have to worry about anything. Besides, once the people at my job found out what happened to me, they were not trying to force me to come back to work. My supervisor told me to take all the time I needed but I knew that wasn't going to last long.

Everyone had been trying to get in touch with me, including Samara. I didn't want to see her because I know if I looked at her, I would see Shane. When I said I told myself I was done with him, I meant it. I didn't want Samara to come here and bring up her brother to me. I was kind of low key mad at her for even setting me up with Shane, but I knew it wasn't really her fault.

"Jayla, I know you're going through a lot right now and you probably don't want to see anybody, but I just want to see if you're doing okay. I miss you at work and I miss you coming over my house to hang out. Remember how we use to drink wine and watch ratchet TV?" Samara laughed on the message she left on my voicemail. "Just think about it. I'd love to come over. I'll bring the pink Moscato." I sighed as I deleted the message. I was about to put the phone on silent, when I saw that Samara was calling again.

"Hi," I said in a low voice.

"Thanks for picking up." I heard the smile in her voice. "How are you doing?"

"I'm doing a little better," I confessed. "How's everything going at work?"

"Who cares about that place?" she blurted out. "How are you?"

"I answered you."

"No, don't give me the typical answer. I want to know how you are doing for real."

"I don't know how to answer that."

"Can I come over?"

I didn't answer her right away because I could feel the word "no" coming out my mouth. I didn't want to push her away. She'd been trying for so long to talk to me and hang out. I closed my eyes and let my heartbeat slow down. I didn't know why the thought of anybody coming over made me so nervous. I knew I was safe.

"Yeah, you can come over."

Ten minutes later, my doorbell was ringing. I took one look in the mirror before I opened it. I put just a little bit of makeup on. I didn't want her to see how horrible I looked. I knew if she saw how bad I really was, she was going to move in with me. I covered up my puffy eyes and added some Chapstick to my lips. I finally brushed my hair for the first time in what felt like years and swept everything into a nice and neat top bun. It's funny how much better you can look after you put some time and effort into it.

"Hey girl." She hugged me softly the second my door opened. I started smiling because it was right then and there that I realized that I really missed my friend. Her optimism always made me feel better. Even this small hug from her made me feel like everything was going to be okay. "And this is the bottle of pink that I promised to bring."

"You used to always bring over pink." I rolled my eyes. "You could try some red or white wine too."

"Girl, you already know I'm too bougie for that. I like my wine pink," she said in a British accent. "It's very classy."

When I started laughing, I stopped. I didn't expect that sound to come from me. It's been so long since I laughed. My whole body started to relax. All the tension I had earlier was gone. The visit with Samara was what I needed. She had me laughing and smiling. At first, she didn't talk about the attack. We talked about work, what was going on with our favorite reality shows, and bullshit that we would see on social media.

"So…" Samara dragged out the word and I knew that the easy part of the conversation was over. It was time for her to really get into why she came over.

"Yeah?" I sipped the wine slowly from the glass not looking up at her. Even though I felt her eyes on me, I just wanted to avoid it for a while longer. As soon as the conversation shifted, I felt the tension come back into the room and my body.

"I figured we could really talk."

"Do we have to?" I asked putting the glass down. "I liked the other conversation better."

"Come on Jayla." She chugged the rest of her wine. "Shane told me some of what happened, but I really don't know the full story."

"What is there to know? Damiah tried to kill me." I took a pause when I felt the tears trying to come out my eyes, but I didn't want to cry in front of my friend. I knew that she was worried, and I didn't need her to be worried even more. "She beat me up, tied me up, threw me in the closet, and planned to burn me and the house up." The story came out of me slowly and when I was done, I took in a deep breath.

It was silent for a little bit. Samara just stared at me with this shocked expression on her face.

"I knew that bitch was a little off, but I never thought..." She didn't finish her sentence. She now had tears in her eyes, but she blinked to stop herself from crying. "I'm so sorry Jayla. I kind of feel that this is my fault."

"To be honest with you, I thought of that, but I know you would never put me in danger on purpose."

"Right," was all Samara could manage to say.

"It's okay," I told her.

"Did you hear the news?" she whispered.

She didn't have to explain further. I knew what she meant just by the tone of her voice. She wanted to know if I knew what happened to Damiah and Trell. I nodded my head and started sipping the rest of my wine.

"I spoke to detectives to give them more details of the incident." I leaned back in the chair. "On my way out, they let me know that they've been arrested."

"Yeah I know. That's good." She tried to smile.

"What's up?" I noticed that she was kind of off.

"Nothing." She was lying. All over Samara's face, it was obvious she wanted to say something else, but she was holding back.

"What's going on?"

"That's what I'm wondering. I know you've told me about what happened to you, but I can't help but feel that there is more to the story."

"What do you mean?"

"It's like you're holding back. Did something else happen at the house that you're not saying?"

"No, I've said everything." My heart started to race and just then, a flash of Darius' face popped in my head.

"But it just seems that something else is there."

I didn't want to tell her about Darius and my past. I couldn't relive holding his dead body in my arms while waiting for the police.

Ever since the whole situation went down with Damiah, some of my nightmares has been popping up again. It was like I was back there with Darius. The look in his eyes still haunted me to this day. This whole thing with Damiah and Trell just triggered everything in me.

"I don't want to talk about my past," I spoke slowly. "I can't go back there."

"Is it bad?" she asked, and I just gave her a look. "I see." She reached out and touch my hand. "You are going to have to tell somebody one day about it."

"Keon knows."

"Maybe other people should know too."

"Are you talking about your brother?" I asked her point blank. I knew it was only a matter of time before one of us brought up Shane.

"Well, why not?"

Samara loved her brother, there was no doubt about that. I remember how her eyes lit up when she talked about him. She was so happy when we first got together. To think about how good everything was back then to the shitty place it was now, was crazy. Life is so full of twists and turns. One day you're falling in love with a man that treats you so good and the next day, you're facing death.

"I love your brother." When I said this her eyes opened wide. "I do. I really do love your brother. I would be lying to you and myself if I didn't admit that I was falling in love with Shane. He's a nice guy and he knows how to treat me. When I was with him, it was like it was only me and him in the whole entire world. I love that man."

"That's good." She smiled.

"But—"

"No!" She interrupted me. "Don't say that. It can't be good if you say that. Let's just leave it at that you love him."

"I do love him, but I can't deal with him anymore."

"But why not? Damiah is going to be locked up for a long time and you don't have to worry about her anymore."

"I just can't deal with the extra drama that comes with Shane."

"But that's over."

"It's never going to be over. Shane and

that chick got a baby together Samara, that's not something that's going to go away."

"But—"

"But nothing." I cut her off. "I love Shane butt I'm not losing my life over Shane."

She opened her mouth to speak but she didn't say anything. She just slowly nodded her head and started to get ready to leave. She said that she was going home and gave me a hug. She told me one more time that she was happy that I was safe.

"Call me when you get home," I said, and she told me she would. But I knew she was lying. She wasn't going home. I had a feeling she was headed straight to her brother's house.

Shane

THE DOORBELL STARTED RINGING like crazy and I ran to answer it. I found my sister Samara on the other side of my door.

"Damn girl." I let her in. "Why was you ringing my bell like that?"

"Because I knew that was the only way you'd come to the door fast enough."

Samara knew me well. With my son with me full time, any time I had to myself, I was going over paperwork for the gyms. After everything went down with my crazy baby mama, I tried to reach out to Jayla, but she wasn't hearing it. So, I just concentrated on work. I was neglecting a lot of people. But I figured if I couldn't hang out with Jayla, there was nothing else I really wanted to do but be with my son and work.

"How are you doing sis?" I asked when I saw her slip her shoes off. She was getting comfortable so that means she had something to tell me.

"I'm good, but how are you? How are you adjusting to being a full-time Daddy?"

"I love it." I smiled, thinking about my son. "It's nice to not have to deal with Damiah. I just wish it didn't have to happen the way that it did." I got real quiet thinking about Jayla. "Have you spoken to her?"

"Who? Damiah? Why the fuck would I want to talk to her?"

"No." I sat down on my couch. "Have you spoken to Jayla?"

Her silence told me her answer. She didn't have to speak. Knowing my sister, she would only be here if it had to do with Jayla.

"It's not good news, is it?" I asked her, and she tried to fake a smile, but then she just shook her head. "So, tell me what's going on?"

"She told me that she loves you, but she can't deal with you anymore."

"She loves me?"

I really wanted to hear those words from Jayla and not my sister, but considering the situation, I had to get it however it came.

"Yeah, she said she loved you, but did you hear the rest of what I said? She said she can't deal with you anymore."

"But didn't' she hear about what happened? Damiah and Trell are both locked up. With all the evidence they collected from this house, they are going to be locked up for a long time. She doesn't have to worry about them anymore."

"Listen, I know that bro. She said that the cops told her all of that already."

"And she still doesn't want anything to do with me?"

"She said that, but I don't know. I got the feeling that there was something else there."

When I looked at Samara and saw her squinting, I knew her brain was at work. Ever since she was kids, she would squint her eyes when she was thinking of something.

"What are you thinking?" I asked her as I watched her in silence.

"I just think that there is something else there." She looked at me and crossed her arms. "It's like there is more to the story."

"You think that Damiah and Trell did something else to her in the house?" I felt myself get angry, but I had to calm down. The police were dealing with those two, so I didn't need to get myself worked up over them.

"You know, I asked her that and she said no. But I don't think it's them, Shane. I think something else happened to her in the past. When I tried to get her to talk about it she shut me down."

"I don't know much about her past either," I truthfully told her.

"Well, I think that's where all this push back is coming from."

After my sister left, I couldn't stop myself from thinking of Jayla. Even when I was working, she still was in my mind. I knew that she needed her space, but it hurt that she didn't want anything to do with me. Damiah fucked up a good thing. There was so much that I wanted to do with Jayla. Before this whole thing happened, I was planning a life for me, her and my son, but now that seemed close to impossible.

I poured myself a stiff drink and gulped it down. I didn't want to let go of Jayla. I knew that woman was special when I first met her. She carried herself differently and that was one of the reasons why I fell for her. I was not going to let her go. I must let her know that she and I could have this great life together, but how could I do that when she wanted nothing to do with me?

Jayla

THE HOUSE WAS quiet after Samara left. Slowly but surely, my depression came, and it put me right back in bed. Samara brought up Shane and a lot of my old feelings came back, but if I was honest with myself, my feelings for him never left. I was staying in bed all this time because I just wanted to sulk and think about Shane. As much as I hated to admit it, I missed him all the time. It wasn't easy to stay away from him, but it was too much.

The whole reason why I moved to Houston was to escape the drama. Darius' murder had me shook and I had to get out. Houston was supposed to be drama free and just a place for a new start. It was going great before I got with Shane. Keon turned his life around and met Crystal and I was doing well too. Now look at it all. I just escaped death over a guy I hadn't even been with that long. This whole fucked up situation with Damiah was just too much. When she first popped up, I should have been gone. I should have left him earlier, but I was always a sucker for love.

As soon as a man made me feel like a million bucks, I stuck around. I stayed in some toxic situations all because I fell in love.

Darius had a whole wife and I stayed because I loved him. Shane had this thing with Damiah and I stayed. I was threatened by his baby mama and I stayed. All these red flags with Shane and all because I fell in love with him, I was stupid enough to stay.

I've always heard the saying that love is not enough, and I finally get it. Love is not enough to deal with the bullshit. I was about to die over love for Shane. I'd decided to stay home and surround myself with family. Crystal and Keon had been with me almost 24/7. It was nice and comforting especially with all that happened. Everything happened fast with me and Shane that I should I have slowed down. Now I had to stay home and take time off work because I was still traumatized. I needed to get my mind right, and fast.

CHAPTER 10

Jayla

Two months passed since the whole situation. I finally got out of bed and started work again. It was weird at first, because my co-workers were acting so differently around me. First it started with whispers behind my back. They didn't talk to me, but I knew they were talking about me. I would walk by them and it would suddenly get quiet. That didn't last long though. A day or two later, they would just talk to me or treat me as if I was fragile.

They'd hug me softly, speak to me softly, and always asked me if I was alright. Now we were in the phase that they were treating me normally, but occasionally, I'd get a look.

Even with the people at my job treating me like an alien, it was still good for me. It helped keep me busy and not to think about Shane. I was missing him badly every single day. It was getting harder and harder not to keep in contact with him. It wasn't until I wasn't calling him that I realized I liked getting his text messages, or his phone calls, and going out on dates with him. I missed touching him, kissing him, and the way he held me. Sometimes I would be home, and I would smell his cologne out of nowhere and I'd get that sinking feeling in my heart. Shane was such a big part of my life and it was not easy to turn all that off. But sadly, as much as it hurt me to stay away from him, it was the safest option. I needed to go back to how I was before Shane. I needed to stay to myself and away from any potential drama.

Damiah's and Trell's court case was coming up and I was getting nervous. The night before the trial, Crystal came into my room. She held hands with me and she prayed for me. She prayed for me to have strength to face them. She prayed that I didn't sink into a depression after seeing them. More importantly, she prayed that justice was served. After she finished, I realized how much we all went through this experience together. Even though I was the one that physically went through it, Keon and Crystal suffered too. When Crystal prayed over me, it reminded me why I loved her so much.

The day of the trial, there was a soft knock at my door. Two minutes later, Keon peeked his head in.

"How are you doing today?" he asked.

"I'm going to be okay," was all I could managed to say.

"Well, Crystal made you some breakfast and whenever you're ready, we're out here for you." He tried to give me his best smile as he left the room. I took a deep breath and got ready for the day.

After dressing up, I took one look in the mirror. I was wearing black and white with my hair up in a bun. In a weird way, it looked like I was dressed for a funeral. I thought about all that could have happened if Damiah and Trell got their way. I shook my head to

shake out all the fears and remembered last
night when Crystal prayed over me. I felt the
strength pushing through and I walked out my
bedroom. Keon was waiting with my car keys
in his hands.

"Okay, let's go."

We got to court early, and the lawyers
brought me and quickly had me seated. I was
so nervous, but I didn't want to show it. I took
in a deep breath and started to scan the room.
I saw Keon sitting in the seat behind me. He
nodded his head and I did the same back.
Suddenly the door opened and in walked
Shane.

It had been so long since I'd seen Shane
that it was almost like seeing him for the first
time. His fit body did that suit justice. His
broad shoulders, his muscular arms, and that
chiseled face drew me in like a magnet. Just
seeing him brought in all the old feelings and
memories back ten times more. It was like just
looking at him, I could feel his lips on my lips
and his hands touching me everywhere. Why
did he have to look so good?

Shane sat close to the back and didn't see
me. He looked concerned and I could tell in

his eyes that he hadn't been sleeping. He looked almost as stressed as me. This situation must have been hurting him too but it all started because of him. Because of his relationship with Damiah we were all here today. This was the reason why Shane and I could never get back together. He was too much trouble.

Not so long after did a door open to the side and I heard metal clinking. It didn't take a genius to know that it was handcuffs. My heart started to race when I saw Damiah walk in slowly. She didn't look like herself. She had these long cornrows and her face looked so dark. She looked over at me and I could have sworn she rolled her eyes at me. She had some nerve. I bet in her head, she still thought this was all my fault.

Right after Damiah, Trell walked in. He looked hardened and he started to look around the room. He looked at me and I tried to read his expression. I couldn't tell if he was sad because of what happened to me or was he angry because he got caught. His eyes shifted and then got focused on one person in the room. I followed his gaze and saw that he was staring at Shane. That was when it hit me. Trell was obsessed with hate for Shane, just like Damiah was with me. In a weird way, they were the perfect match for each other.

"All rise," the bailiff said, and everyone stood up. "The honorable Judge Granger..." He kept talking as the judge walked in and took her seat. She was a middle-aged woman with glasses and her face meant business. After we were seated she took two seconds to look over the papers that were in front of her.

"Let's begin," she said, and the trial started.

The District Attorney started talking about Damiah and her craziness. He brought up the fact that she popped up at my job and then he eventually started talking about that day. He painted the picture so well that I started tearing up. It was like he was right there, and I knew that he got all this information from the detectives. Then he started speaking about Trell and brought up his past. Apparently Trell had been in prison before and the DA was trying to get him locked up for a long time. He kept saying that Trell didn't deserve to be out in society. It was basically time to lock him up and throw away the key.

The defense got up and tried their best. They said that Damiah had mental issues and she blacked out during the attack. They were going to bring in mental experts to say that she shouldn't go to jail because she didn't know any better. They even said that they had proof that I tried to threaten Damiah's life and she was just defending herself. As far as Trell went, they said that he was just in the wrong place at the wrong time. There was no evidence that he did anything to me at all. They even used the information that I gave the detectives when I told them that I never saw Trell there.

When it was my time to get on the stand, the district attorney took my hand and squeezed it softly. He told me a long time ago that I had to prepare to get up there and that it wasn't going to be easy. He knew that it was a lot of stress in this situation and that's why he worked so hard to make sure Damiah and Trell were on trial at the same time. He wanted me to only have to tell my side of the story once and not stress myself out.

"Tell us what happened on the day of question," the DA opened up, and I just told the truth. I told the judge how I was in bed and Damiah just popped in. I told her about the beatings and the whole thing with the fire. The judge kept shaking her head and as I told the story, I could hear people gasping. My voice started to get shaky and I asked for a second to get myself together. The DA got me tissues just as the tears came down my face. Somehow me and Damiah locked eyes and she just rolled them at me again.

The defense got up and walked over slowly.

"I'm sorry that happened to you," the lawyer said. "That sounds very traumatizing."

"It was."

"When you claim that my client Damiah came in, did she say anything to you in particular?"

"I can't remember the exact words that she said."

"Really?" He sounded surprised. "I would think with such a tragic event like that, you would remember every word."

"Sir, I hope you never have anything tragic

happen to you. When something like that happens to you, you try to forget every second. If I didn't try to put it behind me, I wouldn't be able to get out of bed."

"That is understandable." He stopped and then turned around. "Did you fight with Damiah?"

"No sir."

"Did you threaten her life?"

"No sir."

"So, you mean this whole thing went down and you didn't do anything? Are you trying to make us believe that Damiah just picked on you?"

"She wasn't happy with the fact that I was dating her ex."

"Would you say that she took the news of you and her ex dating well?"

"No, I would not."

"Would you say that she went crazy because of the fact you were dating him?" the defense asked. That was when the DA stood up.

"Objection! Your honor, this young woman is not a medical expert, and therefore she can't make an assessment on anybody's mental state."

"Agreed," the judge said, peering over her glasses. "Move on."

The defense attorney kept trying to come at me, but the DA objected every chance that he could. The DA warned me that this could happen, but it was challenging not to break down from his constant questions. He wanted to know about me and Shane. He kept asking questions on whether Shane and I planned to hurt Damiah. Then he said that it was clear that Damiah was provoked and that she blacked out. He said that none of it was planned and that Damiah had a clear record. She had no criminal charges, and this was her first arrest.

"Objection!" The DA shot up and then the judge called them over to her bench. I tried to listen to what they were saying but they were talking very quietly. They walked back and then I was told that I could get down. The trial went on and they kept going over evidence. They showed all the broken perfume bottles and all the things that Damiah was going to light on fire. The DA even had the bullets that they got from the house and they matched to the guns they found on Damiah and Trell. After a while the DA asked for a break because I whispered that I couldn't take it all.

"How are you doing?" Keon asked me when I stepped outside.

"It's just a lot," I told him truthfully. The tears started forming in my eyes. "Just hearing everything and all the evidence." I blew out some air.

"I know," he said through his teeth. I was emotional, but Keon was pissed.

"It's over though." I patted his back.

"I know," he repeated, but his voice was softer. "I just hate that this happened to you."

"Me too."

I looked to the side and saw Shane. He still didn't see me, or maybe he couldn't look at me. We hadn't talked in so long, and I knew Samara told him that I wanted nothing to do with him. All his messages and texts went unanswered. Pretty soon he got the message and left me alone, but it was still nice to see him. He was such a big part of this mess and like me, he needed to know

what was going to happen to Damiah and
Trell.

The trial continued, and it was finally time
for the closing arguments. The DA just kept
talking about the evidence that was against
Trell and Damiah. Both sat there barely
moving or blinking. It was like they were
watching someone else's trial and not their
own. At times Damiah just looked bored and
Trell looked annoyed. One time the judge had
to tell them to sit up straight and they gave her
a little bit of an attitude. It was all unbe-
lievable.

"I have never in my twenty years as a
judge have heard of a case as monstrous like
this. It is not because of the crime but the
blatant disregard of both defendants. Not only
was this young lady Damiah planning to
murder this woman, but she was going to burn
her in the process. She has shown time and
time again that she is not fit to be out in
society or even a mother."

"I'm a good mother!" Damiah suddenly
screamed out. "What you not gonna do is
disrespect me as mother." She sucked her
teeth.

"Silence!" The judge banged her gavel. "You are the one that disrespected yourself as a mother the second you tried to harm this young lady. You are the one that chose this path. You chose to make your son not have a mother in his life. What kind of example of a woman are you? You're just a woman who had a baby. You are no mother at all."

The courtroom was silent as the judge told off Damiah. She didn't look sad or bad while the judge was speaking, but she still had an attitude. She still pretended like she was just at McDonald's waiting for her order. It was like any minute now they were going to hand her food and not a jail sentence.

"As for you, young man, you've obviously have learned nothing from the jail time you did serve. You are a prime example at what happens when soft hearted people meet a hardened criminal. There is no way you should be out with others. You should have gotten out of prison and turned your life around. You should have done anything else than get involved in a life of crime. The fact that not only were you linked to this crime, but drugs were found on you as well is astounding.

You are a disgrace and need to be back into the prison system as soon as possible. I've decided my judgement."

My heart started beating faster. This was it. This was what we were all waiting for. I turned my head slightly and looked at Keon. Crystal was now sitting next to him. She had a test today, but she was finally here. Seeing her here put me more at ease. She gave me a smile and I nodded at her. The judge finally spoke, and when she gave out the sentences for Damiah and Trell, all the air left my body. I went completely deaf as I stood there in shock. She gave both 14 years each and Trell got two extra years because of the drug charge. Finally, Damiah and Trell both lost their minds. Trell started getting up and tried to attack the defense lawyer, but the cops were on him in seconds. And Damiah broke down in tears.

"Your stupid bitch!" she screamed at me. "This is all your fault!" she sobbed.

"Silence!" The judge slammed the gavel down.

"Shut the fuck up." She spat at the judge.

"What are you going to do? Arrest me?" She laughed.

"Young lady, I will hold you in contempt of court."

"You just gave me 14 years! Nothing else matters anymore." She cried and then laughed.

"Take them away."

The trial was finally over, and I gave the DA a hug. He promised me that he was going to lock them up and he did.

"You're finally safe." He grinned at me and then started to walk away. Crystal and Keon gave me a hug and I let the tears out.

"Are you okay?" Crystal asked me.

"These are tears of happiness." I chuckled. "It's finally over." I felt the relief all in my body. All the stress was gone.

Damiah was going to prison for a long time and I didn't have to worry about her anymore. I was so glad that she was going to serve time for what she did and that made my tears of happiness flow. But then I stopped and thought. If Damiah was in prison for that long, by the time she came out of prison, her son would be damn near a man. He might forget all about her and that was kind of sad. I knew how it was like to not really have parents in your life and the last thing I wanted was that to happen to someone else. But the judge was right; Damiah chose this life.

Leaving the courthouse, the sun seemed to shine brighter. The air felt new and clean and it was truly a better day. I turned to my side and saw Shane again. He had his jacket slung over his shoulder and we finally caught eyes. His eyes tried to say what his mouth couldn't. It looked like he wanted to speak but he didn't. He just nodded at me and I did the same. He was probably still dealing with all that just happened. He was truly a single father now and he had someone that is going to need him. I hoped he has all the guidance and strength to raise that boy right. I may not have been with him anymore, but I knew it wouldn't be easy.

"Are you ready to go?" Keon asked jingling the car keys behind me. That snapped me out of staring at Shane.

"Yeah." I was still looking at Shane. "I'm ready to go." I got in the car and closed it door. Shane still stood there looking at me. A part of me wanted to reach out to him and just hug him. Even though most of the hurt happened to me, I knew he was hurting too. But I couldn't touch him though because that part of us was over. The whole thing with Shane and Jayla had to be done for the sake of my safety.

Jayla

We got home, and I immediately went for a glass of wine. For the first time in a long time, I really needed it. Even though I know that Damiah and Trell were gone, I couldn't help but feel worried. I could have died and just hearing all the details brought back the depression. My bed was screaming at me telling me to get back inside. Depression was such a headache to deal with. While you're feeling sad and useless, it's just nice at the same time to be feeling something. I needed to drink this wine so that my depression didn't come back in full force, but I knew it might be a losing battle.

A week later, I took the time off work. I'd run out of vacation time and sick days, so I was taking a risk, but I couldn't get myself out of bed. I just laid there feeling useless. Every time I tried to get up, I'd find a reason to stay in bed. It wasn't the right time to leave the house or I didn't like leaving after the sun went down. Just the look of the night put fear in my heart. It got so bad that I had to have the blinds closed always. I was losing track of time and I couldn't bring myself out of the funk.

The worst part of this depression was that my nightmares came back. One night I would dream about Darius' death all over again. I could smell the blood and see the life slipping out of his body. When I woke up, I was covered in sweat and I would have a tear rolling down my cheek. I thought I would never feel so helpless in my life until the day Damiah came and tried to kill me. Now if I wasn't having these nightmares about Darius, I kept reliving the bullshit I went through with Damiah. The only difference was that instead of me surviving, I woke up after she killed me. I would wake up screaming.

Keon and Crystal were worried about me and so was everyone else. Samara kept trying to get me to come to work, but I just lied and said I didn't feel well. Crystal tried to get me to come out and get our nails done together, like we always use to do. I just would decline and get back to bed. Keon would knock on my door and ask if he could do anything, but I just shook my head. He tried to get me to come out with him too, holding my phone and trying to get me to chase him for it.

"I don't care," I mumbled and went back to bed.

Shane

"Daddy?" my son was in his bed. "When are we going to finish my room?" he asked. I laughed and shook my head. He had his own room filled with all his toys and some new ones. I was trying to make up for everything that happened.

"What is it you want?"

"I want a big poster of Spiderman and Black Panther." He smiled. "And I want one of SpongeBob and Patrick." He laughed. I shook my head.

"But none of that makes sense." I mumbled but I smiled at him. "Okay, it's time for you to go to bed."

"Okay Daddy." I tucked him in. I was almost out the room when I heard him call out to me. "Do you think Mommy likes where she lives now?"

My heart broke. Ever since Damiah's arrest I hadn't really told my son the truth. What was I supposed to say to him? Was I supposed to tell him that his Mommy tried to kill someone? All I managed to tell him is that his Mommy is in a new place. After hearing that Damiah was going to be in jail for over ten years, I knew eventually I would have to tell him the truth. But looking at his big brown eyes and hearing the innocence in his voice, I wasn't ready for that yet.

"Goodnight, son." I turned on his night light and turned off the other light.

My eyes started twitching. They slowly

filled with tears and I blinked them away. I
loved my son, but I know that the rest of our
lives were going to be filled with some sort of
stress because of Damiah's decisions. Sometimes I thought that maybe I could have
prevented it all. Maybe if I told Jayla the truth
from jump, we would have been ready. I could
have sat Damiah down and really talked to
her. Maybe she would have kept a cool head
if I came at her differently. Who knows?

My phone started to vibrate and surpris-
ingly I saw Jayla's number. I couldn't believe
it. When we locked eyes at court, I thought I
felt something there. Samara told me that she
loved me, but my sister also said that she didn't
want anything to do with me. Maybe after all
this time she'd decided that we can have a
second chance.

"Hello," I greeted.

"Hey, it's me, Keon," a male voice said. It
was Jayla's brother. Before the trial, the
hospital was the last time I had seen him. If
looks could kill, I would have been dead.

"How are you? I was just shocked to see
Jayla's number."

"Yeah, I have her phone," he explained.

"How is she doing?"

"Not good." He sighed. "Not good at all. Shane, that's why I called you."

"Me?"

"Yeah, I need your help."

I went to my bar and got out my bottle of vodka. For some reason I knew that I would need it. Taking three quick shots of vodka, I paused and then put the phone back to my ear.

"Go ahead."

Keon coughed and then stopped.

"Look, I'm not going to act like I know what's going on between you and my sister. I don't understand it and after all the bullshit that went down, maybe I never will. But I will say this man, when y'all two was together, my sister was so happy. She would come home smiling and shit, and I knew that was because of you. So, I just need your help."

"With what?"

"My sister is depressed. And I'm not saying that she's a little sad, I'm saying she's really depressed. She practically lives in her bedroom. She bathes only at night. She watches TV but mostly those murder shows, or the criminal investigation shows. She's not the same person. It's like I'm living with a dead body."

Shaking my head, I couldn't believe what I was hearing. Jayla was always so vibrant and always laughing and smiling. To hear that she was depressed made me feel like shit. I already felt like it was all my fault, but I didn't want Jayla to suffer. I was hoping after the trial she would have some peace, but I guess that was not the case.

"I'm really sorry to hear that. I really am sorry. I'm sorry for everything."

"Listen, I use to blame you too, but in court today I saw how crazy that bitch was. There wasn't anything that none of y'all could do. She looked like she had her mind made up about my sister." He was saying things that were truthful, but I still felt guilty.

"But I could have done something."

"You did. Do you realize what would have happened if you didn't come looking for my sister?" I heard the hurt in his voice. "I know I was mad the last time I saw you and a part of me is still upset, but I should thank you. Thank you for what you did for my sister."

When I heard him say those words, I felt a little bit better. I was so busy beating myself up for what happened with Jayla, that I never stopped to think about what I did.

"Thanks." I sipped a little bit more of vodka. "What is it that you need me to do?"

"I need you to come over and help Jayla."

"What? Man, I don't know about that. I've hurt Jayla enough. Besides, she's made it clear that I don't need to be around her and maybe she's right."

"No, she's not. She's not okay and I know you love her—"

"Wait." I cut him off. "How do you know that I love her?"

"Man, Stevie Wonder could see that y'all are in love. I know you love my sister and that's why you need to come and help her out."

"I'm not sure."

"Look, if you love her, you'll be here."

He hung up before I could say anything else. I walked back to my son's room and found him fast asleep. I smiled remembering that there was a time I wanted to introduce him to Jayla. Damn, how times had changed.

~

Jayla

"Is THERE anything I can do for you before I go to class?" Keon peeked his head in my bedroom. I lifted my head.

"Class? What time is it? I thought it was like midnight."

"No Jay, it's like 9 in the morning."

"Oh." I shrugged my shoulders. I swung my legs over the edge of my bed. "I don't need anything. I guess I'll go take a shower."

"You sure you don't want anything?" he asked, and I just shook my head no. "I'll be back right after class, okay?"

"You don't have to keep checking up on me," I told him, but he left without replying to me.

I took my clothes off and went to the bathroom. Opening my bathroom cabinet, I saw the rose scented bath gels that I use to bathe with. Popping the cap open, I took one long whiff. The scent brought back memories of me trying to get ready for my dates with Shane. I used to drown myself with this stuff.

Those days were over though. I shrugged my shoulders and just grabbed the unscented bar of soap and got in the shower. After I was finished, I walked slowly to the kitchen. It had been some time since I had breakfast and I was finally hungry. I opened the fridge and found it to be stocked. I guessed Keon and Crystal was doing all the grocery shopping. Finally deciding on some cereal, I poured myself a bowl and sat down to eat. Before I could put the spoon to my lips, my doorbell rang.

"Coming." I yawned. Keon was always ordering something off the damn internet. Every now and then he would buy some clothes, shoes, games, or whatever he could find off eBay. Besides checking the mail, signing for Keon's deliveries were the other reason I got out of my bedroom. I slowly opened my door and I took a step back. "Shane?" I blinked hard because I could have sworn I was making him up, but there he was.

He had on a sweat suit and immediately his cologne walked into my house.

"How are you, Jayla?"

Had I known that Shane was coming, I

would have looked nicer. All I had on was a ratty shirt and some old leggings. I touched my hair and realized it was in a messy ponytail.

"You look...good." He read my mind. "Is it okay if I come in?" he asked, his voice still as sexy as ever. Without thinking, I moved the side so that he could walk in. His footsteps echoed around this empty house. I saw his head looking at my place. It looked clean but even I could tell that the house had no life in it. "How are you, Jayla?"

"I'm fine," I lied quickly.

"Are you really?"

I was about to lie some more but then I started to cry. Shane hugged me immediately and I cried in his arms. He held me tight and it felt good to be back in his arms. I was reminded of how safe I use to feel here. It was the best place to be and I felt myself getting addicted to his touch again.

"How would you like to take a walk?" he asked out of nowhere. The thought of leaving my house made my heart race, but the look in Shane's eyes let me know that everything was going to be okay.

"Let me just change."

For the first few blocks, we didn't say anything. We just walked in silence listening to the sounds of outside. The cars driving by, people talking while walking past us, and things like that. It was like we were both waiting to see who was going to speak first.

"I can only imagine how things are going for you. I want to say this just to be clear. You know I never meant for you to get hurt."

"I know, Shane. Damiah is crazy and she was going to do anything and everything to me, but you have to understand..." I didn't finish the sentence.

"I have to understand?" I knew Shane was going to want to know the rest of my statement.

"You have to understand that it was very hard to be around you."

"It was very hard *not* being around you," he told me as we stopped at a cafe.

We sat down and ordered breakfast. I watched everyone move around quickly. Our order was done within minutes and we took a seat outside. I was only going to have a crois-sant, but Shane ordered me a sausage breakfast sandwich with orange juice. This would be my first real meal in a long time.

"So, how are you?" I asked him while I slowly bit into my food.

"I'm okay."

"How is it being with your son all the time?" I smiled thinking of Shane in that role.

"It's new. I was used to doing things with Damiah, but this is like what I've been wanting for so long. Now I don't have to worry about whether or not I get to see my son."

"I just wish she didn't have to get locked up for that to happen."

"Me too."

"I wish you the best with that because I know it can't be easy."

"It isn't. My boy got his own huge room and he seems so happy, but then..." He stopped and took a long sip of his orange juice.

"But then you can see that he misses his Mom?" I completed his sentence and he agreed. "You're going to have to take it one day at a time," I suggested

After breakfast, we made our way back to

my house. We didn't talk about much. Shane suggested I get back to work.

"You were always serious about your job," he pointed out as we stood outside my door.

"It was one of the things that I really respected about you."

"I don't know. It just feels weird there."

"Take it one day at a time." He repeated my advice to him back to me.

"You're right," I admitted. "I'll be back there tomorrow."

We stood outside my door just looking at each other. I knew I should go back inside, but a part of me just wanted him to lean in and kiss my lips like he used to. Even though I knew it wouldn't be the smartest thing to do, I just wanted to feel his lips one more time.

"Jayla," he said slowly. "I just want to apologize for everything."

"I know Shane, you've already—"

"May I please finish?" he asked, and I nodded. "One of the things that I hate the most about the situation is that I never got to really tell you how I feel about you. I love you Jayla, I really do. Even with this time apart, I never stopped loving you. You mean a lot to me and I still see a future with you. I want a future with you." He took my hand and held it softly. "I don't want things to end like this. I would like us to start over again. We can do it right this time. I'll take it slow or at any speed you'd like me to, I just want us to be together again."

A smile spread across my face. I didn't even feel it coming, but once it was there it was hard for it come off.

"Shane, I missed you. I really did miss you. It wasn't easy to not be around you." The truth started coming out of me and I couldn't stop it.

"Does that mean we can start over?"

"Shane, I love you, too." His eyes got soft and his smile was so bright. "But——"

"But?" The light left his eyes and his smile started to fade away.

"But," I continued. "I am going to have to think about it."

He didn't say much. He just brought my hands to his lips and kissed them both softly.

"You take all the time you need Jayla. I was serious when I said that you mean a lot to me. I'm going to wait for you." He leaned in and my heart started to race. His lips kissed my forehead and the sparks ran all over my body. He walked away right after that and I watched him get in his car. He honked his horn twice and then drove away.

I leaned against my house door and slid to the floor. I loved Shane, but could I really put myself back there again? Was there more drama waiting for me if I went back? Was I ready to be someone's stepmother?

"What am I going to do?" I asked myself, looking up at the sky.

FIND out what happens next in His Dirty Secret Book 11! Available Now!

FOLLOW Mia Black on Instagram for more updates: @authormiablack

CPSIA information can be obtained
at www.ICGtesting.com
Printed in the USA
LVHW021633120619
621003LV00013B/528